Praise for The No. 2 Feline Detective Agency series

'**Original and intriguing...** a world without people which cat lovers will enter and enjoy.'
P. D. James

'**Deliciously clever and a true delight**.'
Laura Thompson

'**I loved it**. The whole concept is just so "real"!'
Barbara Erskine

'Mandy Morton's Feline Detective Agency instigates a new genre, both **wonderful and surreal**.' Maddy Prior

'The world that Morton has created is **irresistible**.' Publishers Weekly

'Witty and smart. **Prepare to be besotted**.'
M. K. Graff

'Mandy Morton's series is both **charming and whimsical**.' Barry Forshaw

'Hettie Bagshot might be a new face at the scene of a crime, but already **she could teach most fictional detectives a thing or two**.' The Hunts Post

By Mandy Morton

The No. 2 **FELINE** Detective Agency

MURDER ON THE SANTA CLAWS EXPRESS

MANDY MORTON

Farrago

This edition published in 2023 by Farrago,
an imprint of Duckworth Books Ltd
1 Golden Court, Richmond TW9 1EU, United Kingdom

www.farragobooks.com

Print ISBN: 978-1-78842-4-691
eBook ISBN: 978-1-78842-4-707

*For Nicola and all those cats
happy to share a pork pie*

Family Tree

The Stokers

Hornby Stoker

Tender Stoker

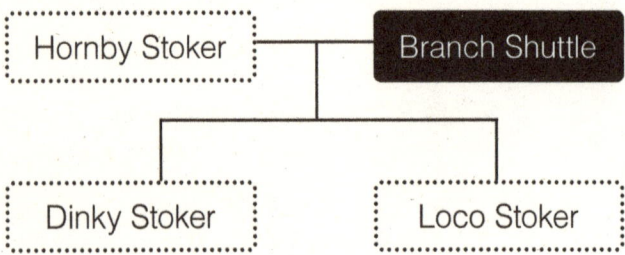

Hornby Stoker — Branch Shuttle

Dinky Stoker · Loco Stoker

The Shuttles

Whistler Shuttle
Branch Shuttle
Waggoner Shuttle

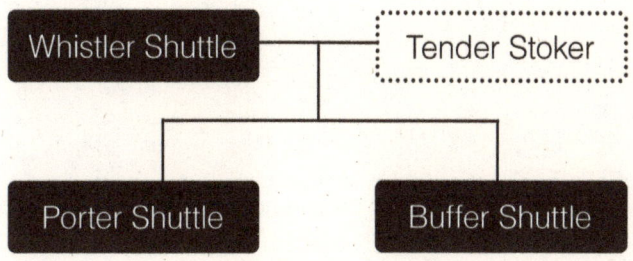

Chapter One
Half a Pork Pie

In Tilly Jenkins's early life, the approach of the Christmas season had never been a happy one. She was barely more than a kitten when her mother took up with a violent tomcat who had used his paws to great effect on her, making it clear that she should leave her family home and try to make her own way in a bewildering world, where being homeless and hungry was a normal state of affairs.

Her first Christmas living on the streets had nearly been her last. She'd been set upon by a band of marauding thugs and left to freeze as they tossed her aside, having taken the only blanket she owned and robbed her of the few pennies she had left from her mother's not-so-generous parting gift.

The library, where she spent most of her days in the reading room, close to a radiator, was closed for the holidays, and all the shops where she often lingered out of the cold had served their final customers tumbling home to indulge themselves in four days of celebration. She remembered how the night sky was full of smoke from the town's chimneys, and how much colder that had made her feel as she imagined happy families gathered round blazing fires, sharing those special treats that the magical season offered.

As she lay shivering and bleeding from her injuries, she had wished with all her heart that death would come and snatch her away from her troubled life. It was Miss Lambert and her adopted daughter, Jessie, who had saved the day by scooping her up and carrying her home to their own fireside, where she had spent the rest of the holiday bathing in their generosity and making the first friends she had ever known. She was keen not to overstay her welcome and no sooner were the baubles back in their boxes than she was on her way, back to the library and her favoured shop doorways at night, promising to return if things became extreme once again.

Miss Lambert was long gone now and had left Jessie her small house in Cheapcuts Lane, where she ran a very successful charity shop, but Tilly remained homeless for several more Christmases before her soulmate turned up one Christmas Eve and shared a pork pie with her in the doorway of the town's department store.

Hettie Bagshot was a resourceful tabby cat. She'd never allowed life to defeat her, even though it had offered more downs than ups, and she had set herself up in an old shed on the Wither-Fork allotments after announcing a break in her relatively successful music career. Her reasons for hanging up her guitar were unclear, but she had settled into a peaceful life of lazy retirement when the Great Storm hit and battered the country, felling mighty trees and creating havoc across the land. Hettie's shed didn't stand a chance and for the first time in her life she was homeless.

Hettie was a cat who always landed on her paws and the arrival of Betty and Beryl Butter – two enterprising cats from Lancashire – saved the day. Betty and Beryl set up a bakery in the high street and very soon the cats of the town flocked through the door, keen to try their delicious cakes, pies and pastries. The bakery was a runaway success, and it was a chance remark from Hettie that brought them even more attention. Hettie had pointed out that Betty and Beryl's pies were far superior to anything sold in the food hall of Malkin and Sprinkle. She had shared her observation with Mr

Malkin himself, who reacted by stocking several items from the Butter sisters' range of delights, firmly establishing them at the heart of the town's food industry.

Betty and Beryl were delighted, and, as a thank you, offered Hettie their unused store room at the back of the bakery – a permanent home for a very small rent, which included coal and a daily pie of her choice. Beryl donated an old armchair, a table and an ancient sideboard to their newly acquired lodger, preferring something a little more contemporary in their own upstairs flat. Hettie's new bolthole was warm and dry, but she was the first to admit that she was no homemaker. Wandering the streets had become a habit and the lack of purpose in her life had made her lonely. She'd never been one for celebrating Christmas, feeling that there was a sadness about it: a festival of excess for the lucky few who could afford it, and for the rest a disappointment; families thrown together who didn't even like each other; the tightening of belts for the rest of the winter to pay for it; and a rather ugly competitive spirit between the haves and have-nots.

That Christmas Eve, Hettie had pushed one of the Butters' pork pies into her pocket and left the comfort of her room to stride out into the snow in search of adventure. She was bored with the cheerful chatter the radio offered and the promise of yet another cat taking on the role of Ebenezer Scrooge for the Christmas Eve drama. The snow had been steadily falling all day and the high street was a total white-out. Earlier, the street had bustled with last-minute shoppers, but now all was silent and deserted. The evidence of Christmas was still to be found in the shop windows as Hettie trudged through the snow; no doubt all that festive cheer would have sale reduction tickets by the New Year, she thought, pulling her cynic's hat down against the cold.

By the time she'd reached the bottom of the high street, she was beginning to wish she had stayed by her small fire. There was nothing of interest to occupy her thoughts. The shop windows of Malkin and Sprinkle were cheery enough, with brightly painted sledges and bicycles. There was even a miniature train set puffing its way around a track lined with model platforms, stations and signal boxes, bursting with tiny cats all seemingly going about their business in an imaginary world. Hettie stood and watched the model train pass her by several times before her attention was drawn to a heap of newspapers in the shop doorway. As she looked a little closer, the bundle of papers moved and a small tabby cat's head appeared and looked at her, blinking.

As soon as Hettie moved, the head shot back into the newspapers and, as she grew closer, she heard a pitiful voice coming from the mountain of newsprint. 'Please don't hurt me,' it said, as Hettie began to peel the newspapers away. 'I'll get out of your way if you want to sleep here, but please don't hurt me.'

'And why on earth would I want to hurt you?' Hettie asked, pulling the final sheet away from Tilly's head.

'Because this is the best place to sleep and cats fight over it, and some cats just like hurting me and I don't seem to be able to fight back.'

Hettie looked down at the small tabby, saddened by what she saw. Her fur was matted and she was perilously thin in all the wrong places, her giant paws making it clear that – with a few decent dinners – she should be a much bigger cat. Her eyes bulged, sticky from several bouts of cat flu, and she shook with cold and the fear of what might happen next.

Hettie slid down next to her and pulled the pork pie out of her pocket. 'This is a bit too big for me,' she said. 'Maybe you'd like to share it?'

Tilly shook her head. 'That's kind, but I couldn't take your food. You might need it tomorrow; there'll be nothing in the dustbins till the new year.'

Hettie laughed and broke the pie in half, forcing the bigger piece into one of Tilly's paws. 'Let's not worry about tomorrow,' she said. 'Let's just sit here and enjoy this pie. After all, it is Christmas.'

Tilly sat up and took a healthy bite out of the pork pie, chewing it very slowly and making every crumb of it last as long as possible. Hettie nibbled at the edge of hers, while Tilly sucked the remaining jelly from around the pork before posting the final piece into her mouth.

'Don't you like your pie?' Tilly asked, noticing that Hettie had made very little progress.

'Actually, I'm sick of them,' Hettie lied. 'I'm going to throw this away – unless you'd like it?'

Tilly took the half-nibbled pie and proceeded to wrap it in a corner of newspaper. 'If you don't mind, I'll save this for later. I can't eat much at once as I'm not used to it – and there isn't usually much to eat anyway.'

Hettie Bagshot could never be described as a sentimental cat. She took life's blows firmly on her tabby chin and expected those around her to do the same, but there was something about the cat in front of her that made her heart ache with the sadness and injustice that had clearly been dealt her. Suddenly, and without warning, she rose to her feet and pulled Tilly up from her bed of newspapers. 'Come on – you're coming home with me,' she said. 'We're going to have the best Christmas we've ever had and you can leave the rest of that pie for the next cat along.'

Tilly reluctantly abandoned the pie as Hettie tugged her out into the snow, heading in the direction of the Butters' bakery and the new life that they would share together from that moment onwards.

These memories came flooding back to Tilly as she fumbled for the cellotape. There was so little time before Hettie returned, and she needed to get this very special gift wrapped and under the tree. It had been months in the making, made all the more difficult by having to keep it a secret. She'd snatched a few hours here and there between their cases, and Betty and Beryl had been wonderful, sitting up late into the night to offer much-needed assistance.

There had been several Christmases since she had moved into their little room at the back of the bakery, but the first one would always be special. Tilly remembered every minute detail: the sudden warmth of the fire as Hettie opened the door to her room; the radio playing out the joyous ending to Mr Dickens's Christmas story; Betty and Beryl showering her with fleecy blankets, and welcoming her as Hettie's new friend; the supper of cold chicken, mince pies, sausage rolls and fiery ginger beer; and the long, uninterrupted sleep without fear of attack from other street cats. The Christmas bells rang out from St Kipper's that Christmas morning to herald in a new life for her, and she hoped that this special gift would say all the thank yous to Hettie that she had never managed to find the words for.

They were going to be busy over the holiday. Since they'd formed The No. 2 Feline Detective Agency, it seemed that they were always busy, such was their success, but Tilly hoped that Hettie would find time to enjoy the precious parcel that now peeped out from under their tree.

Chapter Two
'All Aboard'

'This is not the way I'd have liked to spend Christmas Eve,' grumbled Hettie, as Bruiser pulled away from the station on Miss Scarlet, promising to return to pick them up later. She watched as their motorbike and sidecar disappeared into the gathering snowstorm. 'Why we ever agreed to this ridiculous murder mystery thing I'll never know.'

Tilly pulled the collar up on her business mac and stamped her feet against the cold. 'It's for a good cause,' she pointed out, 'and we both know what it's like to be homeless at Christmas. All the lovely money we raise tonight will bring warmth and shelter to lots of cats who aren't as lucky as we are.'

'Well, I don't see why we couldn't have sent money instead and gone to the same party that Bruiser is heading for. Much better than playing at murder with a bunch of cats who wouldn't know a killer even if they bumped into one.'

Tilly refused to discuss the matter further, knowing that her friend would get more and more cross if she allowed the subject to continue. Instead, she turned to the station entrance where a very large board had been placed by the door announcing a murder mystery evening aboard The Santa Claws Express. A sold-out sticker had been plastered across it, but she was still able to make out what she regarded as being the important bit.

'Look!' she said, tugging at the sleeve of Hettie's mac, 'it says "Come and meet Hettie Bagshot and Tilly Jenkins from the world-famous No. 2 Feline Detective Agency as they set out to catch a killer".'

'Fame at last,' said Hettie, employing her best note of sarcasm. 'I can't think of anything more appropriate than to be sat on an old steam train in the middle of a snowstorm on Christmas Eve with a bunch of would-be Miss Marbles.'

There was no time for Tilly to offer a reply, as the station door was flung open by a plump female cat dressed in crimson-and-cream livery. 'I'm sorry to say that we are completely sold out for our performance this evening,' she wheezed, more than a little out of breath. 'We are expecting the

11

arrival of our special guests at any moment. You're welcome to wait and get their autographs, but I'm afraid that's all I'm able to offer.'

Tilly was curious to know who the special guests might be, but Hettie was in no doubt. 'Do you mean Hettie Bagshot and Tilly Jenkins?' she suggested, 'because if you do, you need look no further.'

The cat before them bent low in some form of reverential curtsey, losing her footing and toppling forward flat onto her face. Hettie and Tilly hauled her back onto her feet. 'Oh, I do apologise. What a welcome! You must think me very silly, but I'm a little awestruck. I've never met anyone famous before – well, I don't *think* I have. I've certainly served a lot of cats in our Biscuit Jar Buffet over the years, but if they don't tell you they're famous, how would you know?'

It was a question for which neither Hettie nor Tilly had an answer, but the mention of a buffet gave them hope of somewhere warm to retreat to. The snow was now falling relentlessly, covering everything – including them – in a thick, white blanket.

'Perhaps we might find somewhere out of this storm?' Hettie suggested.

'Oh my, where are my manners? Please come this way – everyone is waiting to meet you.'

Hettie and Tilly followed the cat through the door of the station and into a very small ticket hall, furnished with bright red leather bench seats that had seen better days, giant radiators, and the smallest of windows into the office itself, where a slight, bespectacled cat sat twirling his whiskers and humming a rather out of tune seasonal medley.

'Time you were changed into your costume, Loco. I've got the detectives here with me, so we'll be off in about fifteen minutes. I'm taking them through to the buffet to meet everyone and do my welcome speech, so you can lock up and get yourself into the guard's van.'

Hettie and Tilly nodded to the cat framed by the ticket office window as they were rushed through by their host, emerging onto a railway platform where a giant steam engine pulling seven carriages stood simmering on the tracks, allowing the occasional puff of white smoke to escape into the snowy night sky. It was a magical scene from a bygone age, and had it not been for the icy blast as they left the ticket office, Tilly would have loved to linger and take in the sight of the giant beast before her. 'It's just like in *The Railway Kittens*!' she cried with delight, but her words were carried away in the arctic wind that howled down the platform.

The station boasted several buildings: a waiting room; the station master's office; a mailroom; and, to Hettie and Tilly's relief, the aforementioned Biscuit Jar Buffet. As they approached, it was clear that there was warmth to be had behind its double doors – the windows were completely steamed up.

Once inside, Hettie realised that they were at the point of no return. The buffet was packed to the rafters with cats, all waiting to greet their distinguished fellow travellers, and a cheer went up as they moved in closer to get their first glimpse of two real-life detectives. Tilly beamed back and Hettie offered an understated nod to the crowd as their host clambered onto one of the Formica table tops and clapped her paws together.

'Welcome to Mogbury-on-the-Tilt Railway Station on this special Christmas Eve,' she began. 'My name is Dinky Stoker, and I am a member of the two families who have run this railway line for over a hundred years.' She paused to allow the crowd to gasp in amazement, but there was no particular response, and she pushed on with her welcome speech. 'The Stokers and the Shuttles are two railway families who have fought hard to keep this station – and several others down the line – open, allowing as many cats as possible to enjoy the steam trains of all our yesterdays. A few years ago, in this very Buffet on Christmas Eve, our two families were at war over a sausage sandwich and a sticky-topped sauce bottle. This incident led to the death of my much-loved father, Hornby Stoker, when he hit the buffers at Hissingford Holt, just up the line from here. That station is now out of service, but they do say that Hornby haunts the line, so that's something to watch out for tonight.'

There was an audible gasp from the crowd. Satisfied this time with the impact of her words, Dinky Stoker continued. 'As two families torn apart by such a tragedy, we decided to combine forces to create The Mogbury Players, performing classic pieces of theatre – mostly written and directed by my good self – in and around the stations and trains that our families own, all in memory of my dear father. We have four miles of track, three stations and two steam passenger trains at our disposal. Tonight, we shall travel on The Santa Claws Express and return on The Mogbury Mallard.'

A cheer went up, but Dinky hadn't quite finished. 'Before our evening begins, I should explain how our murder mystery works. I see that you all have your envelopes. Inside, you will find your tickets with your allotted carriage and seat number, a list of suspects, and a form to fill in to say who you think has done it – the murder, that is. Before you leave the Buffet, you can collect a bag from the service counter containing a mince pie, a sausage roll and a Christmas Cracker. We will be stopping at Pawsome Junction, where we have arranged for some carollers to entertain you, and we will be serving sausage baps and mulled wine, and hot chestnuts will also be available, before we continue on to Hissingford Holt, where you will be transferred to our other steam train for the return journey.

'For the purpose of this evening's entertainment, I shall be playing Lady Pistachio Crumb. My brother, Loco Stoker, will be taking the parts of Lord Artichoke Crumb and the Rt Hon. Hazel Twigg. My mother, Branch Stoker, will play Elsie Slink. Gladstone Slink will be played by my cousin, Porter Shuttle; Countess Fluffalot by my other cousin, Buffer Shuttle; and finally my uncle, Waggoner Shuttle, will take the part of Harrison Binge. As you can see, it's very much a family affair and your train driver, who will be playing himself, is my other uncle, Mr Whistler Shuttle.'

The crowd of passengers looked more than a little confused by Dinky Stoker's cast list, and were obviously trying to grasp the differences between the Shuttles, the Stokers and the roles they were playing, but Dinky pressed on with her instructions. 'Before you get into your carriage, I shall invite you to view a body in the guard's van, and I should tell you that there will be a suspect in each carriage whom our detectives will interrogate in front of you. So now let me introduce Miss Hettie Bagshot and Miss Tilly Jenkins from The No. 2 Feline Detective Agency, who will sift through the evidence and help you all to arrive at the correct conclusion – and I should add that as it's Christmas Eve, The Mogbury Players and our detectives here will be donating all their proceeds to The National Homeless Street Cats' Fund. Prizes of catnip selection boxes will be awarded to the first three cats out of the Santa hat who have correctly named the murderer at the end of the evening.'

There was much jostling as the cats, en masse, attempted to secure their white paper bags from the service counter and only Hettie and Tilly witnessed Dinky Stoker's ungainly climb down from the Formica table top. She excused herself briefly, thrusting the list of murder mystery suspects into Tilly's paw and headed for the waiting room, reappearing several minutes later dressed as Lady Pistachio Crumb – or 'in character', as she put it.

Hettie and Tilly were bemused by the whole concept and were both seriously wondering what they had let themselves in for as they trudged through the newly fallen snow, following the crowd towards the guard's van to view the victim of the drama. As they passed the passenger carriages, Tilly was delighted to see that they had all been decorated with paper chains and shiny baubles hanging from the luggage racks; it was clear that Dinky Stoker and her team had gone to a lot of effort to acknowledge the season and bring some cheer to their customers. The heavy snowfall on Christmas Eve was now becoming the icing on the cake and had created the perfect backdrop for a seasonal whodunnit.

It was like no murder scene that Hettie and Tilly had ever attended. For a start, the corpse was noticeably still breathing and sneezed three times due to the mailbag that had been placed over his head. He lay on the floor of the guard's van in a pool of tomato ketchup, with his paws loosely tied behind his back and apparently dressed in a golfer's outfit, complete with plus fours. An iron golf club was lying next to him, presumably a possible murder weapon.

The crowds gathered around the door to view the murder scene before shuffling off in the snow to find their carriages. Hettie and Tilly lingered, hoping to inspect the body and the scene a little more closely, but were thwarted by the murder victim himself, who struggled to his feet, slipped the string off his paws and pulled the mailbag off his head. As they'd suspected, it was Loco from the ticket hall. The cat blinked at them before pulling off his ketchup-soaked plus fours and revealing his station uniform trousers underneath. To their surprise, he then pulled on an elaborate evening gown in sea green and a fox fur, which he draped around his bony shoulders. He finished off the transformation by jamming a blonde wig on his head – which was distinctly at odds with his fine set of whiskers – and perching his spectacles back on his nose. Seeing Hettie and Tilly's bemused expressions, he grinned. 'Trouble is, we don't have enough females to play all the parts Dinky writes,' he said, 'so I'm playing Lady Pistachio Crumb's great-niece, Hazel. Anyway, I'd better be off. I'm in carriage 4A so I'll probably see you later.'

'Before you go, perhaps you can explain something?' said Hettie. 'I've noticed that the carriages have no corridors and open directly onto the platform.'

'That's right. We spent ages renovating those old carriages and we found some lovely materials to cover the seats.'

'Yes, they look very nice, but I was wondering how we are supposed to move from one carriage to another? We're supposed to spend time interviewing all the suspects.'

Loco Stoker grinned again. 'Ah well, you have to pull the communication cord to stop the train so you can hop along to the next carriage.'

'Every time?' Hettie asked, wishing she'd caught a cold and had stayed at home.

'Yes, unless you fancy climbing out the window and crawling along the roof – not advisable in a snowstorm.'

'But I thought the communication cord was for emergencies?' pressed Hettie.

'It is, but we're not having any of those tonight, so you'll be all right. Now, if you'll excuse me, I've got to wave us off. You'd better get yourselves into carriage 1A as we're about to be on our way.'

Loco Stoker picked up a green flag, gathered the hem of his evening gown in his other paw and leapt out of the guard's van, leaving Hettie and Tilly to slip and slide down the platform to the front of the train, where they settled themselves into the first carriage just as the whistle blew and the train began to move slowly out of Mogbury-on-the-Tilt Station.

Chapter Three
Lady Pistachio Crumb

The carriage was packed with would-be detectives, all excitedly discussing the body they had just viewed, while Dinky Stoker – now in character as Lady Pistachio Crumb – adopted a regal air of detachment from those she regarded as the rabble.

Hettie and Tilly squeezed themselves in next to her, deciding to glance at their suspect list before opening their investigations. Tilly adopted her normal policy of reading the list out loud, mainly because she loved lists but also for the benefit of her fellow travellers. All attention turned to her as she stood to read out the names.

The Cast List

Lady Pistachio Crumb   *Rich, titled and beautiful*

Lord Artichoke Crumb   *The murder victim, and married to Lady Crumb*

The Rt Hon. Hazel Twigg   *Great-Niece to Lady Crumb*

Gladstone Slink   *Butler to Lord and Lady Crumb*

Elsie Slink   *Married to Gladstone, and lady's maid to Lady Crumb*

Harrison Binge   *Friend and caddy to Lord Crumb*

Countess Fluffalot   *World famous psychic and keen golfer*

When Tilly had finished her presentation, Hettie turned her attention to interrogating Lady Pistachio Crumb. 'Lady Crumb,' she began, trying not to laugh, 'perhaps you can tell us why your late husband was in the guard's van on this train, dressed in his golfing clothes?'

Lady Crumb reacted by pulling a lace handkerchief from her sleeve and sobbing loudly into it, gaining some sympathetic murmurings from the passengers. The more they responded, the louder the sobs became, as Dinky offered a totally over-the-top command performance of a grieving widow.

Hettie repeated her question and this time received an answer between the sobs. 'He was travelling to Hissingford Holt Golf Club. They were having their annual Christmas party in the clubhouse, but I've no idea why he was in the guard's van.'

Tilly made a note of Lady Crumb's response and some of the keener passengers followed her in scribbling on the backs of their envelopes. Hettie pushed on with the questioning. 'Do you know of anyone who would want to kill Lord Crumb?'

Lady Crumb let out another loud sob before shocking the carriage with her reply. 'Just about everyone. He was probably the most obnoxious cat you could ever meet. He was cruel, spiteful and just plain nasty and, if someone hadn't murdered him, I'm sure I would have done eventually.'

Even Hettie was surprised at this response, but she followed through with the obvious question. 'Are you absolutely sure you didn't murder him? It sounds to me as if there was no love lost between you.'

'There was no love, but lots of money – that's why I put up with him. Then I discovered that he'd made a will leaving everything to his golfing partner, the Countess Fluffalot, who is also on board this train, so why don't you try accusing her?'

'I'm not accusing anyone yet,' Hettie pointed out, 'and I'm sure that the Countess and I will have a conversation, but I'm interested to know why you're so upset about Lord Crumb's death?'

'Because I am now penniless! My lovely house, my beautiful gardens, even my jewels are all to go to that scheming cat who threw herself at him three times a week in any bunker she could find!'

Tilly did her best to restrain herself from giggling, but the passengers looking on laughed, giving Lady Crumb even more opportunity to play to the front stalls. 'The Countess Fluffalot has the morals of an alley cat,' she continued. 'She pretends to be a psychic, but she couldn't even predict a bus coming unless it ran over her – and she can't play golf without cheating. She keeps a load of golf balls in her handbag to replace the ones she's hit into the rough.'

By now the passengers in carriage 1A were totally animated by Lady Crumb's performance but Hettie felt it was time to move on. The train was progressing at a snail's pace, and she was aware that she had another five suspects to interview before they reached the end of the line at Hissingford Holt. She eyed up the communication cord, remembering what Loco Stoker had told her about stopping the train; it seemed a very odd thing to do, but it was probably no more bizarre than the situation that she and Tilly found themselves in.

In one swift movement she stood up and pulled the chain above the door. The response was instant. With a screech of metal, the wheels locked and the carriage came to a standstill. The passengers were shocked and some panicked, but it was Dinky Stoker who came briefly out of character to explain that Hettie and Tilly needed to move on to the next carriage. Reassured, the passengers turned their attention to their paper bags, concentrating on their mince pies and sausage rolls as Hettie and Tilly clambered out of the carriage.

The drop was a long way down onto the rails, but the deep snow helped and it was only a few paces to the door of the next carriage. Countess Fluffalot herself opened the door for them and Hettie helped Tilly up into the carriage before hauling herself up behind. Whistler Shuttle, who was driving the train, abandoned his engine to release the emergency brake that Hettie had engaged, then resumed the journey towards Pawsome Junction.

Carriage 2A was much the same as the previous one, packed with enthusiastic travellers, some wearing the paper hats they'd found in their crackers, others choosing not to open their bags until Hettie and Tilly had done their work.

Hettie thought it would be helpful to update the passengers on Lady Pistachio Crumb's testimony and called upon Tilly to do the honours.

Tilly pulled her notebook from her mac pocket and offered a brief summing-up of their investigations so far. 'We have just spoken with Lady Pistachio Crumb,' she began, 'and she told us that Lord Crumb was on his way to Hissingford Holt Golf Course for a Christmas party, which is why he was on the train. She said he was a horrid, spiteful cat who has left all his money to Countess Fluffalot. Lady Crumb suggested that the Countess might have something to do with his murder, and that she has the morals of an alley cat and liked to spend a lot of time with Lord Crumb in bunkers on the golf course. She also said that the Countess is a cheat and carries golf balls in her handbag.'

'This is outrageous!' interrupted the Countess. 'Such lies! I was Lord Crumb's golf partner and that is all.'

Tilly sat down and Hettie took over. 'Were you aware that Lord Crumb was going to leave all his money to you? Because if that's true, you're now a very rich cat.'

Before responding, the Countess threw her head back and offered a loud theatrical laugh, much to the amusement of the rest of the carriage. 'My dear Miss Bugshot, you should know better than to believe a word that Lady Pistachio Crumb says. There is no money because she has spent it all on folderols and fripperies. Poor Lord Crumb will go to his grave a bankrupt, and she is to blame. I befriended him, and he took me into his confidence. He told me that his butler, Gladstone Slink, was sweet on Lady Crumb and he had caught them selling off some of her jewels so that they would have enough money to run away together. He said that Slink had made several attempts on his life, including tampering with his muffins by lacing the butter with powdered glass. It is Gladstone Slink you should be talking to. He is your murderer, aided and abetted by Lady Pistachio Crumb.'

'You seem very certain that Slink is the murderer,' said Hettie, 'but are you sure that Lord Crumb was telling you the truth? Lady Crumb seemed to think that most cats would have been happy to murder him, including you.'

'That is nonsense. He was the kindest, most generous, most attentive cat I have ever met. I just knew that if he stayed with Lady Pistachio Crumb it would end in tragedy and I was right.'

'Is that because you're a psychic?' Hettie suggested.

'Of course, and I will tell you another thing – there will be more deaths before the bells ring out on Christmas Day.'

The Countess seemed shocked by her own premonition and there was an audible gasp from the passengers as The Santa Claws Express slid into Pawsome Junction.

Chapter Four
Pawsome Junction

Hettie and Tilly were first out of the carriage, relieved this time to have a platform. Other passengers chose to stay where they were, not wishing to face the biting cold. The snow that had fallen earlier was now freezing and the platform was rapidly turning into an ice rink. Undaunted by the weather, a motley collection of carol singers had gathered to serenade the passengers with some seasonal favourites, but their offerings floated up into the snowy night sky, mostly unappreciated by the cats who remained closeted in their warm carriages. The carollers had positioned themselves next to an ancient old cat who stood roasting chestnuts on a brazier, swathed in a thick scarf that went several times around his neck, with his collar pulled up and hat pulled down over his face against the cold.

At the end of the platform, close to the ticket office, Tilly spied a neon sign and brought it to Hettie's attention. 'Look! It says "Station Buffet". Do you think that might mean a nice hot milky tea and a sausage bap? All those paper bags they gave out have made me so hungry.'

'Let's go and find out,' said Hettie. 'Considering that we're supposed to be the star turns in this seasonal farce, I think Dinky Stoker's hospitality falls a long way short of the mark.'

The two cats slid their way past the carol singers and the chestnut seller and were relieved to find the buffet open. Whistler Shuttle had abandoned his engine and was just ahead of them at the counter, cheerfully whistling 'Jingle Bells'. Tilly noticed that his blue boiler suit smelt of smoke and the Santa hat on his head looked more than a little out of place, but – as she kept reminding herself – it was nearly Christmas.

Several other passengers joined the queue, and when it came to Hettie and Tilly's turn, they were rather surprised to see that it was Dinky Stoker behind the counter, back in her station uniform, wielding a kitchen knife and wearing an apron. The menu was limited to hot sausages, buttered baps and tea or hot chocolate. There was also a saucepan of murky-looking mulled wine with bits of cucumber and apple floating on the top, which everyone in the queue steered clear of. Hettie ordered four sausage baps and two hot chocolates but Dinky waved away her money, finally realising that detectives needed feeding along with the paying public.

Hettie and Tilly found a table for two and tucked into their food, keeping an eye on Whistler in case he showed any sign of leaving for his engine. The last thing they wanted was to be stranded at Pawsome Junction on Christmas Eve. Whistler tucked his sausage bap into the front pocket of his boiler suit and lit his pipe, filling the buffet with almost as much smoke as his engine produced. He sat contentedly sipping a mug of hot chocolate.

'So what do you think of the show so far?' asked Hettie through a mouthful of hot sausage.

'Well, I thought it was going to be awful when Dinky Stoker did her presentation at Mogbury,' said Tilly, 'and the body in the guard's van was a bit silly and not very realistic, but I thought what Lady Crumb and Countess Fluffalot had to say was quite interesting. The passengers seem to be enjoying themselves, so that's the main thing, I suppose, but I'm a bit concerned about the Countess saying there would be more deaths. I don't think we were expecting that.'

'The trouble is, they're overacting and lying,' Hettie pointed out, 'and if the rest of the so-called suspects are going to be like that, I don't see how anyone is supposed to solve this murder mystery. I find the railway family thing much more interesting, though.'

'What do you mean?' asked Tilly, reaching for the brown sauce.

'Well, I think family feuds are fascinating,' said Hettie. 'And what about this Hornby Stoker character – how and why did he crash his train at Hissingford Holt? I'd much rather interview Dinky Stoker about that than try and solve a murder that hasn't happened.'

Tilly was about to discuss the issue of the sausage sandwich, the sticky sauce bottle and the prospect of Hornby Stoker's ghost when Whistler Shuttle stood up and made a brisk and purposeful beeline for the door. They looked across at the counter, where Dinky had wiped down her surfaces and was now changing back into her costume. She tipped the unwanted mulled wine down the sink and hurried towards the door.

'Come on,' said Hettie. 'Let's get this over with.

I assume we're in carriage 3A next. We'll save these two sausage baps for later. I have a feeling that we're going to need them, and there'll be nothing at Hissingford Holt because Dinky Stoker said it was out of service.'

The engine was already building up a head of steam as Hettie and Tilly clambered into carriage 3A to continue their investigations. This time they had been dealt Gladstone Slink, played by Porter Shuttle. Tilly gave a brief overview of the story so far for the benefit of the passengers, then Hettie put her first question to Lord Crumb's butler. 'Mr Slink, as you have just heard, Countess Fluffalot seems to think that you had planned to run away with Lady Crumb and that you have conspired with her to murder her husband. Is there any truth in that?'

Gladstone Slink shook his head. 'I never done nothin' of the sort. Me an' 'er Ladyship don't get on. I keeps out of 'er way as much as possible an' leaves 'er to Elsie.'

'That's Elsie your wife?' asked Hettie, amused by the cat's attempt at a theatrical accent.

'Well, she's not exactly my wife 'cause I already 'ave one, but we've kept company for the past few years in service to the Crumbs.'

Hettie paused her questioning for a moment as a whistle blew loudly and the train lurched out of the station. 'The Countess says that you have tried to murder Lord Crumb on several occasions, including putting powdered glass on his muffins?' she continued.

'Why would I bite the paw that feeds me? The trouble with the Countess is she reads too many of them Agatha Crispys. If you're lookin' for a murderer, look no further than 'er. Lord Crumb used to dread 'avin' to play golf with 'er – she was always throwin' 'erself at 'im. I reckon she clouted 'im with that five iron 'cause 'e rejected 'er. 'E only 'ad eyes for Lady Crumb's great-niece, 'azel Twigg. 'E liked 'em young, see.'

'And did Lady Crumb know about him and Hazel?'

'Elsie said she thought 'er Ladyship suspected somethin', but they were careful, if you know what I mean.'

'So as well as Countess Fluffalot, who else do you think might have had a reason to kill Lord Crumb?' asked Hettie, keen to move on to the next carriage.

'I'm not a bettin' cat, but if I was I'd put me money on that 'Arrison Binge. Don't ask me why, but 'e always seemed like 'e was up to somethin', an' a couple of days ago I overheard Lord Crumb tellin' 'im that there were changes comin' an' that 'e might not need 'im to caddy for 'im anymore.'

'And what was his reaction?'

''E was furious – banged the door on 'is way out. Not an 'appy cat by any means.'

'Do you have any idea what the changes were that Lord Crumb was talking about?' asked Hettie.

Slink shook his head again. 'No idea. 'E didn't mention anythin' to me, except that I noticed 'e'd started bein' careful with 'is money – tight, even, an' Elsie told me 'e owed money to the butcher and the coal merchant, an' he'd stopped 'is mornin' papers. Not that I'm complainin' – that was one less job for me as I 'ad to iron 'em. Thinkin' about it, I s'pose I don't 'ave a job at all now 'e's gone.'

Hettie decided not to discuss Gladstone Slink's employment issues but offered one final question to the butler. 'Why do you think Lord Crumb was in the guard's van?'

'Well, that's an easy one,' Slink said. ''E always put 'is golf clubs in there when 'e was travellin' to the links at 'Issingford 'Olt.'

'But he was going to a Christmas party, not to play golf,' Hettie pointed out.

'That is a mystery, then,' said Slink.

35

Hettie stood up, signalling that the interview was over, and it was Tilly who excitedly pulled the communication cord this time. Once again, The Santa Claws Express came to an untimely stop.

Chapter Five
The Dead Cat's Handle

It was a perilous manoeuvre to change carriages this time, as the train had come to a standstill with a steep wooded ravine on either side of the track. The deep snow had created a magical wonderland, which stood out against the night sky and sparkled in the light that the train gave off. Tilly was first out and scrabbled to stop herself tumbling into the wooded basin below by grabbing on to a branch laden with snow, but the branch snapped, depositing its icy blanket on top of Tilly's head. Hettie caught her just in time as she began to fall backwards into the abyss. As the two cats grabbed for the door to the next carriage, the lone figure of Whistler Shuttle could be seen, still whistling, as he carefully clung to the undercarriage of the train, making his way down the track to release the brake that the communication cord had once again engaged.

There was a feeling of great relief in carriage 4A. The passengers had been waiting for some time for Hettie and Tilly to get to them – and spending it with Loco Stoker dressed as the Rt Hon. Hazel Twigg hadn't pleased them. His rather poor transition from Lord Artichoke Crumb to Lady Crumb's great-niece had challenged their perception of the murder mystery; in this particular carriage nothing seemed believable – especially the bespectacled suspect who sat in a crumpled evening gown, wearing a lopsided wig and nursing the green flag that he'd recently waved out of the window.

Hettie sensed the cool atmosphere of displeasure and called upon Tilly to give her summary so far. That seemed to cheer things up, although it was doubtful that any of these particular passengers would be booking for another of The Mogbury Players' efforts. The train now appeared to be speeding along and Hettie tried to drum up some enthusiasm, hoping that the end of the evening was in sight.

Loco's acting was as bad as his costume. Hettie did her best to tease some sensible answers from him on behalf of the paying public, but his high-pitched pretence at being Hazel Twigg fell almost on deaf ears. In Hettie's opinion, he seemed to have found himself in the wrong play and would have been far more suited to pantomime. When she asked if there had been anything between him – or rather her – and the late Lord Crumb, Hazel seemed completely bewildered.

By now, Hettie was beginning to get annoyed. Tilly had come so close to grief in changing carriages, they were cold and in need of a hot dinner, and the so-called murder mystery had just taken a turn for the worse. The sausage bap she'd forced into her mac pocket had been keeping her warm, but now it had gone cold and she knew it needed eating. The last thing she wanted to do was to risk life and limb again by stopping the train to transfer to yet another carriage.

Hettie's dilemma was taken out of her paws by a deafening screech of the train's wheels as it slid along the tracks, coming to an abrupt halt and throwing the carriage into complete chaos. Several cats had been bucketed off their seats and one had cracked heads with the passenger sitting opposite. Another was having an impressive nosebleed, which she generously shared, covering the cat next to her in blood. The Christmas paper chains that had been so carefully hung from the luggage racks had come down around everyone's ears and the shiny baubles were now rolling around on the carriage floor.

Hettie wondered for a split second whether Dinky Stoker had planned this particular emergency stop as part of the performance, but it was the reaction of Loco Stoker that made her realise that something was very wrong. Loco pulled off his evening gown to reveal his train uniform underneath and sprang for the carriage door. Pulling it open and treating the passengers to an icy blast, he dropped down onto the tracks, now mercifully past the ravine. Hettie and Tilly followed him as he slid his way towards the engine. Cats all along the carriages were hanging their heads out of the windows, trying to see what had brought the train to such a violent standstill, so very different from Hettie and Tilly's scheduled emergency stops.

When the three cats reached the engine, it was a sorry sight. Whistler Shuttle was lying on the floor of the footplate with one paw smouldering on the edge of the firebox. A half-eaten sausage bap lay next to him, along with the Santa hat that had fallen from his head. His body was arched and there was a substantial amount of saliva around his mouth. As the three cats stared at the scene, it was instantly clear that Whistler Shuttle was very dead.

Loco reacted quickly and pulled the body away from the firebox, where the coals were burning brightly. The heat in the engine was a real contrast to the freezing temperatures outside. 'Looks like he had a heart attack or something,' said Loco, stamping Whistler's paw out with his foot. 'Thank goodness for the dead cat's handle or it could have been much worse.'

'What do you mean?' asked Hettie, taking a closer look at the body.

'Well, if a driver is taken ill and lets go of the handle that drives the train, a mechanism kicks in to put the brakes on – otherwise, this train would have kept on going until it hit the buffers at Hissingford Holt, which is the end of the line. Given the speed we were travelling at, that would have been enough to derail the carriages and it could have been fatal for the passengers. We're almost at Hissingford now so I reckon Whistler was starting to slow down anyway before he was taken bad.'

'So what's the difference between this brake and the communication cord?' asked Hettie.

'When you pull the cord, it engages a brake on that carriage. The driver will notice and apply a gentle brake to stop the train and Whistler knew you'd be doing it,' Loco explained. 'What happened just now was that the emergency brake came on, causing the train to stop much more quickly, which is why we were all thrown out of our seats.'

There was now a group of cats gathering in the snow by the engine, wanting to see what had happened. Some assumed that the body on the floor was just another part of the murder mystery. Dinky Stoker, still dressed as Lady Crumb, pushed past them and hauled herself up into the cab. It was becoming a little overcrowded now, as Whistler's body was taking up most of the floor space.

Dinky took a closer look at Whistler before offering a deep sigh. 'He should have retired ages ago, silly cat, but would he listen? It was only a matter of time before his heart gave out and to die in the middle of my murder mystery is almost inconsiderate.'

Hettie and Tilly shot a look at her, amazed by her lack of sympathy. Loco jumped down from the engine and began shepherding the passengers back to their carriages.

'Well, I imagine that Whistler's death puts paid to the evening?' Hettie suggested.

Dinky Stoker looked shocked at the very suggestion. 'In the true spirit of The Mogbury Players, I think the show must go on. It's clear that Whistler died of natural causes, and Loco can take over from him. We're nearly at Hissingford Holt, and to avoid upsetting the passengers, they can all get off and wait in the waiting room while we remove the body to the guard's van on The Mogbury Mallard for our return journey.'

'I suppose that's a plan,' said Hettie, 'but why are you so sure that Whistler died of natural causes?'

Dinky nearly fell backwards out of the cab at Hettie's remark. 'What do you mean? Of course it's natural causes. You can't seriously be suggesting that Whistler Shuttle was murdered?'

'I am,' said Hettie, staring at the half-eaten sausage sandwich and the roasted chestnuts scattered on the floor around the body.

Chapter Six
Countess Fluffalot

Having settled the passengers back into their carriages, Loco Stoker returned to the engine. Stepping over Whistler's body, he took up the handle, releasing the brake and allowing the train to move slowly into Hissingford Holt. Dinky was first out onto the platform, moving along the train and throwing the carriage doors open to encourage the passengers to make their way slowly to the waiting room.

Hettie and Tilly were reluctant to leave the heat from the engine, but they followed on, leaving Loco – now joined by Porter Shuttle (still in costume as Gladstone Slink) – to remove Whistler's body. Porter, who was Whistler's son, was beside himself with grief; as Hettie and Tilly looked back along the platform, he dropped his end of his father's body several times before reaching the footbridge which led to the other platform. There, The Mogbury

Mallard train waited silently to be fired up for the return journey back to Mogbury-on-the-Tilt.

The waiting room, like the rest of the station, was derelict. The red leatherette bench seats were torn, with stuffing and old rusty springs spilling out in places, and the floorboards were cracked and broken, allowing a freezing cold draught of air to fill the room. The beige and brown tiled walls offered no comfort to the passengers as they ventured in from the snowy platform, too frightened to stamp their feet in case they fell through the floor. Instead, they blew on their paws and waited for further instructions.

The news of the engine driver's death had been spread by those who had seen the body, some still thinking that it was all part of the murder mystery. It was left to Dinky Stoker to explain once everyone was gathered together. She clambered up onto one of the bench seats and clapped her paws, calling for silence. 'It is my sad duty to announce that our train driver, Mr Whistler Shuttle, has died of a heart attack,' she began. 'This should not in any way spoil your evening, though, as Loco Stoker, my dear brother, will take over as train driver on our return journey back to Mogbury-on-the-Tilt in due course. I hope we can now continue with our murder mystery, and I suggest that our real-life detectives continue with their questions here in the waiting room, when all the suspects are present. We will then invite you to ask questions of your own so that you may arrive at your conclusions. Under the circumstances, I suggest that our detectives refresh us with their findings so far.'

Dinky looked directly at Hettie and Tilly, who stared back at her, both shocked by her insistence on continuing with her ridiculous game. Hettie was about to have her say on the subject when Porter Shuttle rushed into the waiting room, shouting murder. All eyes turned to him as he blurted out the horrific news. 'It's my sister,' he sobbed. 'She's been stabbed – murdered in her seat.'

The passengers gasped. Dinky Stoker was about to say something when Hettie grabbed her paw and gently but firmly pulled her down off the bench, climbing up herself to address the crowd. 'Please, everyone, stay where you are. There will be no further attempts at the murder mystery, as it's clear that there is a real murderer amongst us. I strongly suspect that Whistler Shuttle, the train driver, is also a murder victim.'

Dinky Stoker was about to protest, but Tilly got to her first and pushed her onto a bench seat as Hettie continued, 'Tilly and I will now go with

Porter Shuttle to see what has happened to his sister. For your own safety, no one is to leave the waiting room. When we return, we will begin a real murder investigation – if any of you have information regarding these deaths, we shall be pleased to hear from you then. I must stress that this is not a game and we are now looking for a killer who could actually be standing next to you.'

The passengers, now in shock, looked from left to right, sizing up the cat next to them as Hettie and Tilly swept from the waiting room, taking Porter Shuttle with them, still sobbing uncontrollably. Porter led them to carriage 2A and it became clear that it was the Countess Fluffalot who had been stabbed. Loco Stoker was standing guard outside the carriage and Hettie sent him to join the others in the waiting room.

Porter was first into the carriage, followed by Hettie and Tilly. The body was sitting upright in the same seat that they had questioned her in earlier. The only difference was that she now had a kitchen knife sticking out of her chest, and the front of her theatrical costume was stained with blood around where the knife had entered. Porter slumped down on a seat opposite with his head in his paws, rocking back and forth in total misery.

Tilly sat down next to him, putting her paw on his shoulder in an attempt to comfort him, while Hettie took a closer look at the body. The face showed no element of surprise and the knife had been driven directly into the heart; the fact that there was hardly any blood suggested that the cat had died instantly, which Hettie thought may – in time – help Porter to come to terms with his grief. 'I'm afraid I need to ask you some questions about your sister,' she said, as gently as she could. 'What was her real name, and did she work for the railway as well as being part of The Mogbury Players?'

'Her name was Buffer, Buffer Shuttle. She was my twin sister and she did a bit of everything on the railway. My dad encouraged us to get involved when we were just kittens, and now he's gone too.'

Porter let out another bout of sobbing and Hettie waited before continuing with her questions. 'Dinky Stoker seems to think that your father had a heart attack – did he suffer with his health?'

'No, he never had a day's illness in his life. Strong as an ox, he was. I just can't believe he's gone. What am I going to do without them? All I have left now is Uncle Waggoner and Aunt Branch.'

'And they are also involved in the murder mystery?' asked Hettie, trying to recall the cast list.

'Yes. Waggoner is playing Harrison Binge and Branch is Elsie Slink, but I don't think you've got to them yet,' said Porter, wiping his nose on his sleeve.

'So that means that your aunt was playing your wife, who wasn't really your wife, in the Christmas mystery?' Tilly suggested after checking the cast list.

'That's right,' said Porter. 'We're short of females in the two families to play all Dinky's parts, so Branch got a non-speaking part as Elsie Slink.'

'Why doesn't she speak?' asked Hettie.

'Because she's a bit batty and can't remember her lines but Dinky likes to include her mother in all her plays.'

Hettie and Tilly were becoming confused by all the family connections. It felt strange to have such a conversation in the same space as a dead body, but Hettie pushed on, preferring not to return to the much more public waiting room. 'I know this must be really hard for you, having just found your sister. We will find out who killed her but we're going to need your help.'

Porter nodded. 'I'll do anything I can to help, but I just don't understand why anyone would want to do this to Buffer. She was the sweetest cat you could ever meet.'

'You say that your Aunt Branch is Dinky Stoker's mother,' Hettie continued, 'so explain to me how the family works.'

Tilly sat poised with her notebook as Porter did his best to explain his family tree. 'Well, Aunt Branch was married to Hornby Stoker so they were the parents of my cousins, Dinky and Loco. Tender Stoker – my mother – was also Hornby Stoker's sister and she married Whistler Shuttle, my father.'

At the mention of his father, Porter collapsed into another bout of sobbing. 'I'm sorry,' he said eventually, 'but I can't believe that my dad and Buffer are dead.'

'I completely understand,' said Hettie, 'but we need to draw up a list of suspects and their connections to each other.'

'Suspects!' said Porter. 'Surely you don't believe that the family's involved?'

'I'm afraid I do. In my experience, they often are in cases like this, which is why we need your help. You mentioned your mother – Tender, I think you said? Where is she?'

Porter looked down at his snow-covered boots and allowed two giant tears to fall from his eyes and splash onto them. 'She killed herself a few years ago – jumped off the footbridge, just as The

Mogbury Mallard was pulling out of this station. My father was driving the engine, but there was no time to stop. He never really recovered from that.'

'Why did she do that?' Hettie asked.

'I don't know and I don't think we'll ever know. She'd been really sad after her brother Hornby died, so maybe that was it. She never left a note or anything like that. Dinky reckons she slipped while waving to my dad, but I don't think it was an accident – I think she meant to do it.'

Hettie thought for a moment. It seemed odd that so many of the Shuttle family were dead, but time was ticking on and she needed to learn a lot more about the two families before they returned to the waiting room. 'Tell me about Hornby Stoker and his accident – what happened, exactly?'

'He hit the buffers, in a manner of speaking,' Porter replied. 'I shouldn't speak ill of the dead, but he wasn't a very nice cat. Quite cruel, in fact, especially to my Aunt Branch. That's why she's like she is – a bag of nerves who forgets everything. I think sometimes it hurts too much to remember.'

'So how did Hornby die?' Hettie pressed.

'He fell into his own firebox and burnt to a crisp on Christmas Eve a few years back. By the time Loco found him, there was nothing left but ash. He had it coming to him, that's for sure. He'd had a terrible row in the Biscuit Jar Buffet with my dad that day. He was the worse for drink, and he jumped into one of the engines and took off. It all ended here. They do say he haunts this station, but I've never seen him.'

'Dinky said the row was about a sausage and a sauce bottle,' Hettie suggested.

Porter shook his head. 'It was about much more than that. My dad had put up most of the money when he and Hornby bought the railway and the trains. They were old school friends and they decided to go into business together when the old railway came up for sale. There had been railway workers in both their families for as long as anyone could remember, so I suppose they decided to carry on the family tradition. They'd married into each other's families, and when we all came along, as soon as we were old enough, we helped out to make the railway a success. The trouble was Hornby Stoker was a drunk and a gambler, and the night before that Christmas Eve he'd met some of his cronies in the Mogbury Arms and nearly gambled the railway away. Whistler, my dad, turned up just in time and cancelled the bet. Hornby took off and turned up drunk in the Buffet the next day and he started chucking sausage baps around. My dad squirted him with a brown sauce bottle before Hornby slouched off down the platform and fired up The Mogbury Mallard. Loco was in the guard's van and travelled all the way to Hissingford Holt before he could get off. Luckily, we had no passengers, as the station was closed for the Christmas holidays.'

'Why was Loco in the guard's van?' Hettie asked.

'Because that's where he lived. He loved trains so much that he'd made himself a bedsitter. He moved out after Hornby died, as he said that Hornby's ghost walked the train and this station. Now he lives in the signal box at Mogbury-on-the-Tilt with his sister, Dinky.'

'So Hornby's death was a drunken accident?' Hettie summarised, keen to be clear on the subject.

Porter nodded. 'Although I think he might have killed himself.'

'What makes you say that?'

'Well, several cats came looking for him after he died – threatening types they were, all saying he owed them money from the gambling. They backed off when they found out that he was dead, but I reckon things got too hot for him and he bailed out before they could get to him. He was a coward as well as a bully.'

Hettie glanced back at Buffer Shuttle's body. 'When we interviewed your sister as Countess Fluffalot, she mentioned that there would be more deaths before Christmas Day. Was that part of Dinky's script to excite the passengers?'

'It wasn't in the script I had,' said Porter. 'It was always going to be just the murder of Lord Crumb, but Buffer often knew things.'

'What do you mean?' asked Hettie.

'She had a sort of sixth sense. She saw things in the future; our mother did, as well. Everyone in the family just laughed at Buffer, but I believed her. She took to her bed the day before our mother died, because she said that something terrible was going to happen – and it did.'

'Dinky wrote that into your sister's role on purpose, then? I think she called her a world-famous psychic.'

'Actually, Buffer insisted on that,' Porter pointed out. 'She thought it might make her more interesting as a murder mystery character. Buffer should have been writing the plays, really – she was so much better than Dinky at making up stories, and she was a good actress. The female Shuttles were big music hall stars in Victorian times. It's in our blood. With the exception of Dinky, the Stokers can't act for toffee. Loco is terrible; that's why he always plays the body. Branch Shuttle was on the stage before she took up with Hornby, but he ruined all that for her.'

'Dinky Stoker mentioned that The Mogbury Players were formed to heal the family feud; do you think it has?'

Porter shook his head again. 'Not really. If anything, it's made things worse, as Dinky seems to be running everything now. Since Hornby died, she thinks she owns the railway and all of us with it. My dad Whistler let her take over the general day-to-day stuff because all he wanted to do was drive the trains – that was his passion. He was never happier than when he was in his engine, puffing away on his pipe as the countryside flew by.'

Porter suppressed the sob which rose in his throat at the mention of his father and stared down at his boots again.

'What will happen to the railway now that Whistler has gone?' Hettie asked gently.

'I hadn't thought that far ahead. To be honest, after what's happened, I don't think I'll be staying on. It feels like my family has been wiped out and at the moment I don't care if I never see another train again.'

'I completely understand, but we must make some arrangements for getting your sister's body back to Mogbury. Would you like us to move her into the guard's van on the other train?' Hettie offered.

'Thank you,' said Porter, fighting back the tears. 'That would be very kind and at least she'll be with my dad.'

Hettie stood up in front of the body, screening it from Porter, and gently pulled the knife out of Buffer's chest, then passed it to Tilly, who wrapped the blade in her handkerchief and pushed it into her satchel. The two cats lifted the body and Porter opened the carriage door. Hettie and Tilly carried the cat out onto the snowy platform doing their best to avoid the icy stretches and Porter led the way to the footbridge.

The Mogbury Mallard stood on the opposite platform – a considerably more up-to-date steam train, with interconnecting carriages of a much grander style than The Santa Claws Express. The guard's van at the back of the train was kitted out with bench seats, carpet and even a small sink. Whistler Shuttle's body was already laid out on one of the seats and Hettie and Tilly put their burden down on the other. Porter lingered in the doorway, totally distraught as he took in the scene. There in front of him were the two cats he had loved most in all the world, taken from his life by a murderer's paw. Desolation overwhelmed him as Hettie and Tilly gently steered him back over the footbridge where his mother had ended her life, and once again the snow began to fall.

Chapter Seven
Dinky and Loco Stoker

By the time that Hettie, Tilly and Porter reached the waiting room, it looked a little more welcoming. Someone had had the sense to light a fire in the old fireplace and the passengers had settled themselves in groups on the floor and the old benches, some contentedly finishing off the food in their paper bags. Dinky Stoker greeted Hettie at the door, announcing that the best plan would be for everyone to board The Mogbury Mallard and return to the Biscuit Jar Buffet, where they could be much more comfortable.

Unlike the Shuttle family, Hettie refused to allow Dinky to dominate the proceedings and very publicly put her in her place. 'Murder is never comfortable,' she began, 'and there is a murderer in our midst, so no one leaves this waiting room until we get to the bottom of why Whistler and Buffer Shuttle have been killed – and by whom. I would like to use a separate room for my investigations so where can you suggest?'

Dinky looked more than a little put out, but pointed her paw in the direction of a hatch in one of the walls. 'Through there is the old station master's office. You can reach it from outside, but I still think we'd be better off going back to Mogbury-on-the-Tilt.'

Hettie ignored her last comment and went to investigate the room next door. Except for the cold, it was a perfect place to sift through the suspects. There was a desk, several chairs, an old typewriter and a disconnected telephone. The walls were adorned with framed photographs of train engines, carriages and happy smiling cats – family members, Hettie assumed, as they were all wearing the cream-and-crimson uniforms. The wastepaper basket under the desk was full of bits of paper, and – more curiously – the shells of several chestnuts.

Hettie shivered and glanced across at the old fireplace. Surprisingly, the battered coal scuttle standing next to it had coal and sticks in it and there was a box of matches on the mantelpiece. She laid the sticks and lit them, piling a shovel full of coal on the top, then returned to the waiting room to collect Tilly and their first suspect. She'd already made her mind up to ignore the passengers and concentrate on the Stokers and the Shuttles; with that in mind, she called upon Dinky as their first interview.

Dinky appeared, indignant at being singled out, and slumped down in a chair with more than a little bad grace. Tilly retrieved her notepad from her mac pocket, now covered in brown sauce from the sausage bap she'd saved for later, and Hettie sat behind the station master's desk to look as intimidating as possible.

It was only three hours before the midnight Christmas bells would ring out across the land and it was Hettie's intention to be back in their room at the back of the Butters' bakery with the case solved by then. She relished the challenge, and had already formed a number of possibilities in her mind which she was keen to put to the test. She decided to take the direct approach with Dinky. 'I believe that Whistler Shuttle was poisoned,' she began, 'and I think the poison was in his sausage bap, or possibly in the chestnuts he'd been eating. It's clear from the body that it was a very painful death – the fact that he was bent double with saliva around his mouth confirms that. Only a short while before we observed him being very active out on the tracks, releasing the communication cord brake and showing no sign of illness. His son Porter has confirmed that he had no problems with his heart and was fit and strong. Did you poison his sausage bap?'

Dinky threw her paws up to her face, offering a look of shocked horror before giving Hettie the answer she was expecting. 'No I didn't! I don't know how you dare suggest it! Why would I put all my passengers in danger to do such a thing? You must be mad.'

'But surely you knew about the dead cat's handle?' Hettie suggested.

Dinky looked flustered. 'Of course I did, but I've never known it to be needed on any of our trains.'

'Not even when your father, Hornby Shuttle, burned himself to death?' Hettie countered.

'I don't know about that. I wasn't on the train that night. All I know is that it was a terrible accident. I think Loco tried to spare me the details – he found him.'

'Let's get back to the sausage bap,' said Hettie, pleased to see that Dinky had been rattled. 'You served Whistler in the buffet at Pawsome Junction so you could easily have slipped something into his food.'

'Well I didn't – and you've got no proof, anyway.'

'What did you do with your kitchen knife after you'd finished serving in the buffet?'

'I suppose I left it on the draining board at Pawsome Junction.'

Hettie gave Tilly the nod. She pulled the knife from her satchel and laid it on the desk in front of Dinky Stoker.

'Are you sure you didn't stick it into Buffer Shuttle's heart after we'd found Whistler dead?'

Dinky got to her feet. 'I don't have to sit here and listen to this,' she said. 'I employed you to be part of my murder mystery evening and now you sit there accusing me of a double murder. I know nothing about a poisoned sausage bap or a kitchen knife being used as a weapon and, as the owner of this railway, I'm asking you both to stop all this nonsense and leave us alone.'

'I thought that Whistler owned the railway?' Hettie suggested.

'He did, but now he's dead I'm the obvious one to take over. I inherited my father's share anyway, and all Whistler wanted to do was drive trains. I had to do all the organising. It was just a big game to him.'

'What about your brother, Loco? Shouldn't he have a share? And then there's Porter, Whistler's son.'

'Loco and I are very close and have always shared everything. Porter isn't interested in the railway and that sister of his was bone idle, too – fancied herself as a playwright, and she was always changing my scripts. Obviously, someone got fed up with her – probably one of the passengers.'

'You don't seem at all saddened by these two deaths in your family. There's obviously a lot of bad feeling still between the Stokers and Shuttles in spite of The Mogbury Players. I thought that was supposed to unite you all?'

'I just tell the passengers that. The truth is, I can't stand the Shuttles. They drove my father to his death and tried to steal his railway from him, so whatever happens to them I say good riddance. Now, if you'll excuse me, I'd like to get back to my passengers.'

'That's fine,' said Hettie, 'but no one is going anywhere until I've spoken to all your family members, so if you'd be kind enough to send Loco in next that would be helpful.'

Dinky swept out of the office with an almost triumphant air about her, as though she felt that she had dealt rather well with Hettie.

'That was all very interesting,' said Hettie, adding more coal to the fire. 'As I thought, there's been a civil war brewing between the Stokers and Shuttles for some time and Dinky Stoker is right in the centre of it.'

'I suppose I should put her down as chief suspect after all the nasty things she's said about her family,' Tilly suggested.

Hettie shook her head. 'No, I don't think she's murdered anyone, even though she had the opportunity in both cases. I think there's more to this than plain malice, which she has in spades. I'm not saying she isn't involved, but I don't believe she's a killer.'

Loco Stoker blew in from the platform, bringing a flurry of wet snow with him. He crossed to the fire to warm his paws before sitting in the chair that Hettie offered him.

Tilly found a clean page in her notebook, and Hettie began to quiz the cat in front of her. 'After discovering Whistler Shuttle's body on the train, tell me what you did next.'

Loco shrugged off the question, before giving a short answer. 'I just got the passengers settled back in the carriages so that I could take the train into Hissingford Holt.'

'And did you meet or see any other family members while you were doing this? In their carriages or out in the snow?'

'Not that I can remember. Dinky was in the engine with you. I vaguely remember that Porter was out on the tracks, and I think I caught sight of Waggoner sticking his head out of a carriage window, but it was chaos – cats all over the tracks and the howling wind blowing snow everywhere. It was hard to see anything, really.'

'Did you actually get into any of the carriages?'

'No. I just made sure that everyone else did and then I came back to drive the train into the station.'

'So you didn't see Buffer Shuttle at that point?' Hettie pressed.

'No. The next time I saw her was after me and Porter had moved Whistler's body to The Mallard – we were on our way back to the waiting room. She was just sitting in the carriage. Porter went in to fetch her, and that's when he found her dead. Terrible, really, for him to find her like that, and so soon after Whistler,' said Loco, staring uncomfortably at the knife on the desk.

'How did you get on with Whistler?' Hettie asked.

'Quite well, I suppose. He did hog the trains a bit – I didn't get much of a chance to drive them after my dad died.'

'Why was that?'

'Well, my dad stood my corner with Whistler. He raised me to drive trains and made sure I did. I even lived on The Mallard for a bit, but after his accident Whistler took over the tracks, in a manner of speaking, and left me and my sister to do the boring stuff on the railway.'

'So now Whistler is dead, you'll be the chief train driver on the railway?' Hettie suggested.

'I hope so, but I hope you're not suggesting that I got rid of Whistler to get his trains off him,' Loco objected, looking more than a little frightened.

Hettie ignored the comment and decided to focus her next question on Hornby Stoker. 'You mentioned your father and I gather that you were on the train when he died. Tell me what happened that day.'

Taken aback by Hettie's switch from Whistler to Hornby, Loco looked down at his boots and the puddle of iced water that they'd made on the floor. 'That was the worst day of my life,' he said eventually. 'I was living in the guard's van on The Mallard at the time and I'd been into the Buffet at Mogbury to collect my supper. My dad and Whistler were having a set-to, so I grabbed a couple of sausage rolls and a hot chocolate and took them back to the van. Next thing I know, my dad's rushing past my van on the platform. Then a short time later the train began to move. I thought he was just letting off steam, if you'll pardon the pun, so I sat back to enjoy the ride. When we got to Hissingford Holt, I waited a bit, then got out and walked down the train to the engine to see what dad was up to. When I got there, I couldn't believe my eyes. He'd fallen into the firebox, and all that was left of him was a load of blackened, charred remains and his watch and chain – this one, in fact.' Loco pulled a pocket watch from his uniform waistcoat and put it on the desk next to the kitchen knife.

Hettie picked it up and turned it in her paw. The casing was blackened and the hands were stuck on a quarter to twelve. 'It's a shame it doesn't work,' she said, passing it back to Loco.

'I've never tried to get it to work. I feel closer to my dad knowing that this was the moment he died,' Loco explained, putting the watch back in his waistcoat.

'So did the train actually crash into the station that night, or did Hornby stop it before he died?' asked Hettie.

'To be honest, I didn't notice. There's always a bit of a jolt when it hits the buffers, and I just didn't think about it until I reached the engine. I was so horrified at what I saw that scene has never left me. I still have nightmares about it. It was a horrible accident.'

'What made you think it was an accident?'

'What else could it have been?' said Loco, more than a little alarmed. 'I hope you're not suggesting he was murdered? There was no one else around and I was the only one on the train. Of course it was an accident.'

Hettie decided to let Loco's words hang in the air before changing the subject. 'Who decided to close down Hissingford Holt as a working station?'

'Dinky did. With my dad gone, we didn't have enough of the family to keep it open, so she decided to treat it as the end of the line for changing over the trains. Anyway, after his death we didn't feel much like being here for long. My mother and him lived here. They had an old carriage that they did up – all mod cons, parked in a siding by the footbridge. It's still there, as far as I know. When dad died, my mother moved back to Mogbury. She moved in with Whistler, her brother, and she looked after him in her own way.'

'What do you mean by that?' interrupted Hettie.

'My mother lives on her nerves and she's quite reclusive. She just seems frightened of everything.

Dinky does her best to bring her out of herself by trying to include her in everything, but she's not a happy cat. I don't know what will happen to her now that Whistler's gone.'

'And where was your mother on the night Hornby died?'

'She was back at Mogbury, helping out in the buffet as far as I can remember.'

Hettie recalled what Porter had said about the relationship between Hornby and Branch but decided not to raise the subject with Loco. Instead, she introduced Tender Shuttle into the conversation. 'Were you around when Porter and Buffer's mother died?'

Loco was surprised to be asked about yet another family disaster and said so. 'You seem to know an awful lot about us. I suppose Porter's been filling you in. Yes, I remember the day she died. She'd never quite got over my father's death – they were very close as brother and sister – and I think that's why she jumped off the footbridge, but no one knows for sure. Poor old Whistler suffered, though, as he finished her off by driving his train over her. He just couldn't stop in time.'

Tilly, who'd been frantically scribbling in her notebook, winced as the picture of Tender Shuttle under the wheels of Whistler's train forced its way into her mind.

'Do you find it odd that so many of the Shuttles are now dead?' asked Hettie.

Loco shrugged his shoulders again. 'I suppose it's just the luck of the draw, or us Stokers are made of sterner stuff.'

His comment was a little too light-hearted under the circumstances, but Hettie decided to bring the conversation to an end. 'Perhaps you'd be kind enough to send Waggoner Shuttle in next?' she said.

Hettie waited until Loco had shut the door behind him before discussing him with Tilly. 'It seems to me that Loco Stoker and his sister have got this family railway business sewn up. All these deaths are so convenient, but I don't think either of them is capable of cold-blooded murder, even though they both stand to benefit. There's something I'm missing here. It's staring me in the face, but I just can't see it.'

'I'm looking forward to meeting Branch Stoker,' said Tilly. 'She sounds the most interesting of the lot.'

'Yes, I think you're right,' agreed Hettie. 'Maybe we'll learn more about this family feud from her, and she connects the families together – she's Hornby Stoker's widow and Whistler Shuttle's sister, as well as being Dinky and Loco's mother if I've got that right. It also seems to me that several members of these two families would have been happy to kill Hornby Stoker. Any one of them could have concealed themselves on that train, shoved him into his own firebox and escaped before Loco got to him – and that cat could easily be the killer we're looking for now.'

It was some time before Waggoner Shuttle arrived to be questioned and Hettie and Tilly used the pause in their investigations to eat their cold sausage baps. Although they filled a gap, Hettie was quick to point out – through a mouthful of bread – that it was very poor fare for Christmas Eve. There were now only two hours to go before Christmas Day and Hettie was keeping her claws crossed that there would be a breakthrough in the murders so that they could enjoy it – but time was running out.

Chapter Eight
Waggoner Shuttle

Waggoner Shuttle was the spitting image of his brother – so much so that Hettie thought for a second that Whistler had risen from the dead as he lurched in through the door.

'Sorry I've kept you waiting,' Waggoner said, taking the chair that Hettie offered, 'but this has all been a terrible shock, especially for my sister Branch. They left it to me to break the news to her and it's not easy telling someone that their brother and niece have just died. I'm having enough trouble dealing with it myself, but telling poor Branch was just awful.'

'How did she take it?' Hettie asked.

'It's hard to say. I don't think it's sunk in yet. My sister has one foot in the past and another in the present. Some days she's on top of things; others, she harks back to being a young cat just starting out. She was on the stage, you know, before she got tangled up with Hornby Stoker.'

'I gather that wasn't a happy relationship?' said Hettie.

'He was all sweetness and light to start with, but then he took to gambling and drinking. He fell in with a bunch of local cut-throats and poor Branch suffered for it. Crushed her spirit, he did, but he idolised Dinky and Loco – spoilt rotten, they were. He called them his little railway kittens – when he was sober, that is. Best thing that could happen to him, being incinerated in his own engine.'

'No love lost between you and Hornby, then?' Hettie observed. 'Dinky Stoker seems to think that his ghost haunts the railway.'

'I wouldn't put it past him, but I think Dinky says that for dramatic effect for the benefit of the passengers.'

'Where were you the night Hornby Stoker died?' asked Hettie, keen to explore her theory.

'Well, that's an unexpected question,' said Waggoner, looking slightly disturbed. 'I was in the station master's office at Mogbury. Whistler had asked me to look at the accounts, as he thought there were some mistakes in the orders for the buffet. I did see Hornby stagger past the window, though. He was in a right state, and that was the last time I saw him.'

'How do you get on with the Stokers?'

'All right, I suppose. I'm a part-timer on the railway, so I don't have a lot to do with them. I live in Mogbury and run my own business, so I just help out now and again – and Dinky always writes a part for me in her murder mysteries. That's why I'm here tonight.'

'What business do you run?'

'I'm an undertaker. Things have been a bit quiet lately, although I suppose I'll be busy now with poor Whistler and Buffer, and this cold weather's bound to bring some business in.'

'Could you just run through your journey from Mogbury this evening to where we are now, including any observations you might have made along the way?' asked Hettie, doing her best to ignore the keenness with which Waggoner hoped for a lucrative new year.

'Well, as you know, most of the family were costumed up and I was playing Harrison Binge in Dinky's mystery so she put me in carriage 6A, next to the guard's van. I had a jolly crowd in there. All the passengers were in high spirits and keen to get on with the mystery. We had several stops along the way – I suppose that's when you were changing carriages – but it's a shame you never got to us. I was looking forward to doing my bit of acting. Anyway, several of my passengers got out to stretch their legs and visit the buffet at Pawsome Junction, and when they got back in we all had to make room for the old chestnut seller who wanted a lift to Hissingford Holt. He brought some hot chestnuts with him, so we shared them out and he sat squashed up in the corner until we were all nearly bucketed out of our seats. I thought there'd been a collision or something. I think it must have frightened him, as he was first out of the carriage to see what was happening. My passengers were quite shaken by it all, so I checked that they were all right and then I put my head out of the window to see what was happening. That's when I saw Loco on the tracks, trying to get everyone back on the train. I had no idea that Whistler had died until one of the passengers who'd got out of the carriage came back and said so. He seemed to think it was part of the murder mystery, but I knew it wasn't and I was about to go and see for myself when the train started to move again. It was only a couple of minutes before we reached Hissingford Holt.'

'And did you see the chestnut seller after that?'

'No, but to be honest I wasn't looking for him. I was too shocked and upset about Whistler. Dinky was on the platform, saying she wanted everyone off the train and into the waiting room, so that's where I went. When I got there, I noticed that my sister Branch was missing so I went back to 5A to fetch her. She was all on her own in the carriage and she was in a right state, even before I gave her the bad news. I think she'd been shaken up by the train stopping.'

'Did you know that Buffer was dead at this point?' Hettie asked.

'No. I'd only just broken the news to Branch about Whistler when Porter came into the waiting room shouting murder.'

'I'd like to talk to the chestnut seller if he's next door in the waiting room, but before that perhaps you could fetch your sister Branch for me?'

'I doubt you'll get much sense out of her, but I'll fetch her. I don't think I'd recognise the chestnut seller. He was swathed in a hat, coat and scarf, but you could ask Dinky. I imagine she booked him.'

'Why do you want to talk to the chestnut seller?' Tilly asked, as Waggoner went outside and banged the door behind him.

'Because he doesn't fit in with the families or with the passengers, and he may have seen something that no one else has. He's a wildcard, if you like, and Whistler might have been poisoned by the chestnuts rather than by the sausage bap – they were all over the floor of his engine.'

'Shall I add him to my suspects list, then?'

'Definitely,' said Hettie, 'at least until we've spoken to him and had a chance to rule him out.'

Minutes later, Waggoner Shuttle returned with a frail elderly cat and introduced her as his sister, Branch Stoker. Hettie got up from behind the desk and put out a chair for Branch by the fire, pulling her own up alongside.

'Do you need me any more?' Waggoner asked. 'There's no sign of the chestnut seller in the waiting room. Dinky says he lives on the streets, selling matches in the summer and chestnuts in the winter for a few bob. She said he was begging at Pawsome Junction last week so she gave him a chance to sell his chestnuts on the platform for the Christmas specials. While you're talking to my sister, I'll have a look round the station to see if he's bedded down somewhere if you like?'

'Thank you, that would be really helpful,' said Hettie, pulling up another chair by the fire for Tilly.

The cat before them was strangely dressed in a maid's outfit, with a coat thrown over her bony shoulders, and it reminded Hettie that her role on The Santa Claws Express was to play Lady Crumb's servant, Elsie Slink. 'I'm so very sorry for your loss,' she began, 'but I would like to ask you a few questions, if that's all right?'

Branch began to twist her paws together nervously. 'I'm no good at questions,' she said, almost to herself. 'I haven't got the answers, you see, and if I don't hurry up I'll miss my first entrance and then where will we be?'

Hettie could see instantly that interviewing Branch Stoker was going to be an uphill struggle, but she persevered, going along with the confused world that Branch inhabited. 'I don't think you need to worry – the play has been cancelled for today.'

'Then I'd better get on home to cook Whistler's dinner. He'll be in from the railway soon. I've got a nice chop for his supper and an apple sponge for afters.'

Hettie shot a look at Tilly. She was about to abandon the interview when Branch got to her feet and began pacing the room as if she was completely on her own. At first, she hummed a tune, then she suddenly began to speak to herself. 'I've told you not to be frightened,' she said. 'He can't hurt you because he isn't there. If you sing a song, he'll disappear. If he doesn't stop, you'll have to tell

Whistler and he'll put a stop to it. He won't make me jump, not like Tender. She never came back.'

Branch's conversation with herself was interrupted by Dinky Stoker, who entered the station master's office looking furious. 'I'm sorry,' she said, 'but all this detective stuff has got to stop. My mother isn't up to your interrogations. I don't know what Waggoner was thinking of, subjecting her to this – she hasn't been in her right mind for years. I've got a train load of passengers in the waiting room, all wanting to go home for Christmas, and it's blowing a blizzard out there. You two are making more of this than you need to. I still think Whistler died of a heart attack, so I just don't see what you're trying to prove – and knowing Buffer, she probably stabbed herself by mistake. She's always been accident-prone.'

Branch continued to pace the floor, oblivious to her daughter's intervention, and Hettie decided to put Dinky Stoker firmly in her place. 'Regardless of what you think, there have been two murders on this railway tonight and I suspect that there have been others along the way, passed off as accidents or suicides. Forming a rather amateur theatre company to paper over the family cracks is just a smoke screen for what's really happening here. I suggest that you are fully aware of who the murderer is and you were hoping that, by inviting Tilly and me to host your murder mystery evening, you could distract the other members of the family from the truth. I believe that you are involved up to your neck in a conspiracy that has been going on for years.'

It was as if Dinky had been turned to stone. She stood in silence, digesting Hettie's accusations before finally finding the words to create some form of defence. 'You know nothing about my family,' she began, 'and you have no idea how hard I've worked to keep it together, dealing with all the petty jealousies, obsessions and insanity.' At this point she shot a look at Branch, who continued to pace the floor and mumble to herself. 'I'm now going to get Loco to fire up The Mallard so that we can get the passengers back to Mogbury. I will make sure you are paid for your services regarding the murder mystery and it's up to you whether you donate your fee to charity. That's an end to it.'

Dinky took Branch by one of her paws and led her to the door. Hettie and Tilly watched them as they shuffled out onto the snowy platform, a well-timed gust of wind shutting the door behind them.

'Well, you certainly rattled her cage,' said Tilly, 'but what do we do now?'

'We button up our macs and go and catch a murderer,' Hettie replied.

Chapter Nine
Blood on the Snow

As Hettie and Tilly left the station master's office, they bumped into Loco Stoker, who seemed in a bit of a hurry. 'Can't stop,' he said, doing the buttons up on his boiler suit. 'Dinky wants me to fire up The Mallard for the home run. It's going to take some time to get some steam up in this cold, so I'd better get on.' Loco pushed past them and Hettie watched as the cat made his way along the platform and over the footbridge.

'We'd better get on too,' Hettie said. 'There's not a minute to lose if we want this case wrapped up by the time that train is ready to leave.'

'So do you know who the murderer is?' asked Tilly.

'Yes, I think I do – but it's finding them and proving it that's our problem, and the answer lies somewhere on this station. We need to search all the buildings on the platform and The Santa Claws Express itself, and if we have no luck there we'll do the same on the platform opposite.'

'Who are we looking for?' asked Tilly.

'A cat who sells chestnuts. You start by checking the carriages and I'll take a look at some of these old buildings. Be careful, though – this killer will stop at nothing to get what he wants.'

Tilly started with the engine that had so recently been the scene of Whistler Shuttle's murder. The firebox was still glowing and she was tempted to linger out of the cold, but Hettie had made it clear that there was no time to waste, so she moved on reluctantly down the train, getting in and out of the carriages, towards the guard's van.

The train looked sad with Christmas decorations scattered across the floor of the carriages. There were one or two mittens and hats that the passengers had left behind, and a sea of the white paper bags that had been plundered earlier on the journey from Mogbury-on-the-Tilt. The bags reminded her that she was hungry, and she struck lucky in carriage 5A, where Branch Stoker had been sitting. There were two unopened paper bags and she forced them into her satchel, knowing how pleased Hettie would be to have one of them.

There was something else in the carriage that drew her attention: it was an abandoned scarf and she was certain that she'd seen the chestnut seller wearing it on the platform at Pawsome Junction. It was strange to find it in 5A though, as Waggoner Shuttle had said that the old cat had travelled from Pawsome Junction in carriage 6A. Thinking that the scarf could be a vital piece of evidence, but not quite knowing why, Tilly grabbed it and completed her search of the train, then went back along the platform to look for Hettie.

The blizzard was blowing hard, almost lifting Tilly off her feet. Snow piled up, making it difficult to progress on foot, and it was extremely cold. She bent her head against the wind and hugged the old railway buildings on the platform, pulling open the doors as she looked for Hettie. She passed the waiting room and the station master's office, which seemed to be the only buildings on the platform that weren't completely derelict. Some of the others were open to the sky in places, and carpeted with snow. The old station signs rattled and clanked in the wind, straining on their fixings, and some lay bent and twisted on the ground, having made a successful bid for freedom. The platform seemed to be acting like an arctic wind tunnel, offering no shelter as the snow drifted to form strange ghostly shapes that rose up and died with every icy blast.

The Santa Claws Express looked dark and threatening now against the blanket of white – black and brooding like a giant beast – and Tilly found the deserted platform unsettling. Then she saw the blood and stopped dead, not daring to go any further. Until that moment, it hadn't occurred to her that Hettie might be in danger. The violent red streak had spread out across the snow like an incoming tide and Tilly's life flashed before her as she took in the stain that seeped across the platform towards the silent train.

'I'm afraid Waggoner is done for,' came a voice from behind her. 'I was just too late to save him.'

She turned to see Hettie, larger than life and covered in snow, and threw herself at her friend in sheer joy and relief. 'I thought you'd been murdered!' she cried, sobbing into Hettie's mac. 'I don't think I could ever manage without you.'

'You don't have to,' said Hettie, 'but we do have a job to do, so stop crying and follow me.'

Hettie was about to slide off along the platform but Tilly stopped her. 'Wait! I found this in carriage 5A, where Branch was sitting. I'm sure I saw the cat with the chestnuts wearing it at Pawsome Junction.'

Hettie took the scarf and gave a satisfied nod. 'I'm sure you did, and this proves that Branch Stoker isn't as bonkers as Dinky would like us to believe. Come on, all will become clear very soon.' Hettie pushed on through the snow with Tilly close behind. There was no time to stop and ponder over the body of Waggoner Shuttle, lying in the doorway of the old station café with his throat cut from ear to ear.

Chapter Ten
Home in time for Christmas?

At the end of the platform, close to the footbridge, were some old engine sheds. A signal box rose above them and behind was a siding, where an old and very dilapidated carriage stood. The fall of snow had softened all the old neglected iron-mongery around it and a giant pile of old sleepers lay across the tracks in front of the carriage.

There was a sheer drop of several feet off the end of the platform. Hettie went first and helped Tilly down behind her. Here, away from the wind tunnel, tracks were faintly visible in the snow, together with a trail of blood that the blizzard had yet to cover. The trail led them to the door of the old carriage, and the handle was covered in blood. To Hettie's relief, the knife that she presumed had killed Waggoner was lying discarded in the snow, where the killer had hastily abandoned it.

'We're relying on an element of surprise,' she whispered, looking around for a suitable weapon and finding a rusty iron bar sticking up in the snow. 'Take this and stand by the carriage door. I'm going in. If the killer tries to escape, let them have it – but make sure it's not me before you lash out.'

Tilly stood by the carriage, the iron bar raised and ready to strike, as Hettie reached up and turned the handle on the door. It creaked on its old hinges, but Hettie leapt up into the carriage, giving the cat inside no time to react. He was sitting on a bunk, licking the blood from his paws, still dressed in the coat he'd worn on the platform at Pawsome Junction. He looked up, startled by his visitor, but made no to attempt to move and Hettie decided to take control of the situation immediately. 'I should tell you that this carriage is surrounded, so please don't attempt an escape because you won't get any further than the carriage door – and that relies on your getting past me first.'

'Who are you?' demanded the cat. 'You can't come busting your way in and making threats. Get out while you still can and leave me in peace. I was just looking for some shelter. You wouldn't begrudge me that on a cold winter's night, would you?'

'You certainly seem to have made yourself at home,' said Hettie, taking in the faded but comfortable surroundings. The carriage was almost welcoming, with a small kitchen at one end, two bunks and a stove with a chimney that rose up through the centre of the roof. On the other bunk was a collection of unsold chestnuts, spilling out of brown paper bags. 'Looks like you've had an accident with all that blood on your paws,' she continued, 'although it's not the first time, is it?'

'What do you mean?' asked the cat, stiffening as if getting ready to pounce.

'I mean that there have been lots of accidents this evening. There's the cat lying dead on the platform, the train driver and his daughter, and at least one other tragedy not so long ago – although some say that was a suicide. The thing is, they were all Shuttles, even if Tender Shuttle was originally a Stoker.'

The cat stood up defiantly, rushing at Hettie, who sidestepped him and swung the carriage door open for him to make his escape. Tilly's aim was straight and true as she brought the iron bar down on his head. The cat lay sprawled in the snow, holding his head in his paws.

'I think we'd better have a little chat,' said Hettie, pulling the injured cat to his feet. 'Let's go back inside the carriage and out of the snow.'

The cat gave no resistance, still nursing his head with one paw. He used the other to pull himself up into the carriage, followed by Hettie and Tilly, and returned to the bunk where he'd been sitting. Hettie and Tilly sat opposite him, moving the chestnuts onto a table between them.

'That's a very odd sort of chestnut,' Hettie said, looking more closely at one of them. 'It's the shape, and if I didn't know any better, I'd say it was a conker. Not the sort of thing to get mixed up, is it? Chestnuts are lovely, but conkers – well, they're very poisonous, aren't they?'

The old cat glared at Hettie. 'I don't know what you're getting at or who you are,' he hissed.

'Forgive me,' said Hettie, 'and let me introduce myself. I'm Hettie Bagshot from The No. 2 Feline Detective Agency and this is my assistant, Miss Tilly Jenkins. We have been engaged by Miss Dinky Stoker, who I think you know very well. She has asked us to solve a murder and that is why we're here.'

'And why would Dinky do that? She couldn't have known…'

The old cat's response tailed off and Hettie leapt in to finish it for him. 'She couldn't have known, because you'd planned to keep her out of it and protect her, hadn't you, Mr Hornby Stoker? But she's her father's daughter and I think she knows very well what you've been up to.'

'What are you talking about?' protested the old cat. 'Who on earth is Hornby Stoker?'

Tilly was just as shocked as the old cat in front of them at Hettie's revelation, and she was keen to hear her friend's reasoning. Hettie didn't disappoint. 'Well, let's put some flesh on old charred bones,' she began. 'A few years ago, there was an unfortunate incident in the engine of The Mogbury Mallard. It was on Christmas Eve that Hornby Stoker rowed about the railway with his brother-in-law, Whistler Shuttle, and took off on The Mogbury Mallard in a fit of pique. My guess is that there was another cat in the engine at the time, possibly a street cat who sold chestnuts, as opposed to conkers. I think that old cat had been sheltering in the engine out of the cold. Hornby Stoker drove the Mallard towards Hissingford Holt, and on the way disposed of the unfortunate street cat by incinerating him in the engine's firebox and reducing him to ash. On arrival at Hissingford Holt, Stoker left the train, leaving his watch and chain in the ashes for his son, Loco, to find. Loco was living in the guard's van at the time and was quickly upon the tragic scene, believing his father to be dead. I daresay you watched his grief unfold, perhaps from the station master's office?'

The old cat was about to interject, but Hettie held her paw up to him. 'Please don't interrupt. I haven't quite finished, and neither had you, because the next thing that happened was your sister's suicide, although I suspect you may have helped her fall from the footbridge in front of the train that Whistler Shuttle was driving. Did she discover that you were still alive? In any event, it was a perfect act of revenge against Whistler, getting him to run over his own wife. Then things become a bit sketchy. I'm not sure when your daughter Dinky discovered that you were still alive, but your wife Branch sensed that you were very much around. In fact, I believe you taunted her on the train this evening, disguised as a chestnut seller. She said as much when I talked to her earlier, but I digress. Not satisfied with taking Whistler's wife from him, tonight you embarked on the ultimate plan – to dispose of

Whistler himself by dressing up as the chestnut seller and selling him roasted conkers on the platform at Pawsome Junction. When Whistler collapsed in his engine and died from eating one of the conkers, the chaos that ensued gave you the opportunity to stop off in the carriage where Branch Stoker was sitting to frighten her, or maybe you intended to finish her off and were interrupted. Then came your big mistake: you left your scarf in her carriage, which ruined your disguise. As you got out of Branch's carriage and moved along the platform, Buffer Shuttle recognised you from her carriage window, which meant that she had to die. The trouble with one murder is that it so often leads to more to cover up the first, and just now, when Waggoner Shuttle came looking for the chestnut seller, his luck ran out too. I wonder whether Dinky is next on your list? I'm sure she knows far more about these murders than is good for her.'

The old cat's hackles were up and Hettie expected him to strike out at any moment, but instead he crumpled. 'I would never harm a hair on her head,' he said, adopting a pathetic tone, worthy of the Mogbury Players. 'She's all I have and she doesn't even know I'm still alive.'

Hettie was about to contradict him when the carriage door was nearly wrenched off its hinges as Dinky Stoker burst in. 'Come on, Dad, we're leaving for...'

She suddenly froze, unable to finish her sentence, while Hettie and Tilly stared at her from their bunk. 'Well, well,' said Hettie. 'I rest my case. I think that wraps things up nicely and just in time for Christmas.'

Hornby Stoker stood and leapt for the door before Hettie or Tilly could stop him. Dinky was ahead of him and the two cats jumped from the carriage into the snow. Hettie and Tilly reached the open door in time to see father and daughter make their escape up onto the platform and from there to the bottom of the footbridge. The two detectives followed in pursuit as The Mogbury Mallard released a head of steam into the frosty night on the other side of the bridge. The train was clearly ready to leave and Hettie and Tilly wasted no time in scrambling up the steps and along the bridge. They'd almost caught up with Hornby and Dinky when Hornby slipped on the ice and toppled headfirst onto the tracks. Dinky reached out to save him, lost her footing and tumbled after him just as Loco Stoker released the brake on The Mogbury Mallard.

As with many traumatic events, Hornby and Dinky Stoker's deaths played out in slow motion while Hettie and Tilly watched, powerless to do anything. They were only yards away when the two cats fell onto the rails below. For a split second, Dinky lifted her head from the tracks, her face contorted in horror at the realisation that the giant engine was about to run over her. Hornby Stoker's body lay broken beside her and – as he disappeared under the wheels of the train – Dinky's scream filled the night air, then was suddenly silenced as the engine swallowed her up too, like a whale consuming a sprat. The screech of brakes was deafening when it came, giving The Mogbury Mallard the final word on the deadly game played out by the Shuttles and Stokers.

It was a Christmas that the train passengers would never forget. The murder mystery that they'd so joyfully set out on had ended in total carnage. There was nothing festive about the sombre journey back to Mogbury-on-the-Tilt; it was hardly surprising, as there were five bodies in the guard's van and limited staff on the rest of the train. Loco Stoker insisted on dragging the bodies of his father and sister from under the wheels, more out of anger than shock at their deceit. He had already mourned the passing of his father for several years, but now he had to come to terms with the lies that his sister had told him and the wicked family conspiracy that she and Hornby had created between them.

Bruiser was waiting with Miss Scarlet to take Hettie and Tilly home, and remarkably, by midnight, they were by their own fireside, eating the contents of two paper bags. Needless to say, they wouldn't be roasting chestnuts as part of their festive celebrations.

With most stories at Christmas, there has to be a happy ending, and not only was it yet another triumphant case for The No. 2 Feline Detective Agency, but a little further down the line – if you'll pardon the pun – Loco Stoker and Porter Shuttle joined forces and set up a charity to create permanent homes for local street cats on board both their trains, with free walk-in cafés at all three of their stations. Branch Stoker returned to the stage and to The Royal Shakespaw Company, where she has recently been giving her Lady Macbeth to rapturous audiences.

'The big question is – who murdered Lord Artichoke Crumb?' asked Tilly, adding an apple log to the fire.

'Now that really is a mystery,' said Hettie, filling her catnip pipe.

THE END
(but not quite…)

Chapter Eleven
Half a Pork Pie

Hettie closed the book quietly with great satisfaction, not wanting to wake Tilly, and wiped a tear from her eye. She read the card again that Tilly had written to go with the book, and felt guilty at unwrapping her present even before the first light of Christmas Day had sneaked in through their window. So this was why Tilly had been so secretive for the past few months: she had written a murder mystery just for Hettie and Hettie had to agree it was a good one.

Now it all fitted into place. Tilly's insistence that they visited their local steam railway several times over the summer. Her constant scribbling in a new notebook that she'd bought from Lavender Stamp's post office. Betty and Beryl's late-night typing marathons that came thumping through their ceiling into the early hours, and Tilly's endless visits to Dorcas Ink's printing works in the high street. A conspiracy to create the best Christmas present that Hettie had ever received. A personalised murder mystery to sit back and enjoy without lifting a paw to solve it. She turned the book over, admiring the bright red cover and the gold lettering. It was with a great sense of pride that she traced the title with her claw: *Murder on the Santa Claws Express* by Tilly Jenkins. *'A Hettie Bagshot Mystery'*.

Hettie glanced into the fireplace, laid ready to put a match to it, and smiled to herself. There on a plate was half a pork pie and a glass of sherry, a tradition that Tilly had insisted on for every Christmas they'd spent together, and a reminder of the very first thing they had shared at the beginning of their friendship. Christmas brought with it its own magic, but, as Hettie looked round their room at the sparkly tree, the paper chains, the stockings at either end of the mantelpiece and the holly on the staff sideboard, she realised that without Tilly there would be no magic.

Acknowledgements

The author wishes to thank the Helston, Bodmin and Nene Valley Railways for the lovely days out, the cream teas and their dedication to the bygone age of steam. Also to Betty and Beryl Butter for their secretarial skills, sausage rolls and mince pies, and to Dorcas Ink for the loan of her magnificent printing press and Jammy Dodgers.

Thank you to Pete Duncan, Sarah Lambert, Catriona Robb and all at Farrago, Jason Anscombe for the cover design and Sue Howlett for adding the branches and twigs to the family tree.

About the Author

Mandy Morton was born in Suffolk and after a short and successful music career in the 1970s as a singer-songwriter – during which time she recorded six albums and toured extensively throughout the UK and Scandinavia with her band – she joined the BBC, where she produced and presented arts-based programmes for local and national radio. She more recently presents *The Eclectic Light Show* on mixcloud.com. Mandy lives with her partner, who is also a crime writer, in Cambridge and Cornwall where there is always room for a long-haired tabby cat. She is the author of The No. 2 Feline Detective Agency series and also co-wrote *In Good Company* with Nicola Upson, which chronicles a year in the life of The Cambridge Arts Theatre.

Twitter: **@hettiebagshot** and **@icloudmandy**

Facebook: **HettieBagshotMysteries**

Also available

Cat Among the Pumpkins

As All Hallows' Eve approaches, Hettie and Tilly of The No. 2 Feline Detective Agency have more than just warlock tarts on their plate. When they discover the body of Mavis Spitforce, they must set out to investigate an old crime and a spate of new murders.

Why was Mavis Spitforce dressed for Halloween? Can Irene Peggledrip really talk to cats from the spirit world? And what's the connection to the legend of Milky Myers, suspected of murdering his family on Halloween, longer ago than anyone can remember?

As the November fog closes in, can the tabby duo unearth the truth and stop the murderer before they strike again?

Coming Soon

The Suspicions of Mr Whisker

Hettie Bagshot and Tilly Jenkins are hired to investigate a spate of mysterious deaths at Mr Whisker's Academy for Wayward Cats.

Before Tilly even opens her notebook, the hockey mistress is brutally murdered on the playing field.

Faced with an increasing body count, our feline detectives sharpen their claws and set out to catch a serial killer. Did Pomadora Moseley really murder her family on the rollercoaster at Butlins? Is Clara Toddlebury's Country Dance Class under threat? And why does Mr Whisker lock himself in his headmaster's study?

Join Hettie and Tilly as they chalk up another case, revealing a school full of scandal, a dormitory of death and the latest Butters' pie filling.

Note from the Publisher

To receive updates on new releases in The No. 2 Feline Detective Agency series – plus special offers and news of other humorous fiction series to make you smile – sign up now to the Farrago mailing list at farragobooks.com/sign-up.